Audrey L & Audrey W

&

Best Friends-ish

Audrey L & Audrey W

BOOK 1

Best Friends-ish

Written by
Carter Higgins

Illustrated by
Jennifer K. Mann

chronicle books · san francisco

Library of Congress Cataloging-in-Publication Data available.

ISBN 978-1-4521-8394-7
Manufactured in China.

Design by Jay Marvel.
Typeset in FF Scala.

10 9 8 7 6 5 4 3 2 1

Chronicle Books LLC
680 Second Street
San Francisco, California 94107

Chronicle Books—we see things differently.
Become part of our community at www.chroniclekids.com.

For Taylor N.
—C. H.

For HT, ET, NT.
Thank you for always cheering me on.
—J. K. M.

MS. FINCASTLE'S LITTLE CHICKENS

Dear Room 19,

October has been a *stupendous* month, hasn't it? We got not one, but TWO new friends in Room 19—and only one was an actual second grader! We had some magnificent adventures together, don't you think? I definitely do.

These stories were some of my favorite things that happened in Room 19 this month. Read them in the bathtub. Read them to a tree. Stay up past your bedtime and read them with a flashlight!

Just be careful if you read them in the car, okay? Remember what happened to Diego in the back row of the bus on the way to our whale-watching trip? Please use your common sense.

Here's one more giant shout-out—to you! Thanks, little chickens, for all of your hard work in making Room 19 the best neighborhood around. We'll switch jobs in November!

Line Leader: Wesley

Librarian: Lena

Paper-Passer-Outers + Collectors: Bettina + Von

Most Responsible Scientist: Diego

Plant Waterer: Goldie

Assistant Coaches: Sonya + Charlie

Mini Ms. Fincastle: Kadir

Computer Technician: Mimi

Street Sweeper: George

Newscaster: Jamie

Caboose: Sage

Recycling Boss: Henley

Litterbug: William

Postal Clerk: Isabella

~~On Vacation~~ Welcome Ambassador: Audrey

Love,

Ms. Fincastle

PS: Have you seen my glasses?

CHAPTER 1

At the beginning of the school year, Audrey had been super-duper-duper sure that SECOND grade would be twice as fun as first.

She was ready.

She'd remembered the best parts from first grade, like snack time and the sunny yellow paint on the door and Diego's jokes that sometimes made her snort.

Surely second grade would have all of those things plus better, cooler, *older* things. Second graders even got to put on a whole play, with costumes and everything.

But second grade was not that great yet.

It definitely had all kinds of *new* things. New things like grades on spelling tests and Coach Mallory's contests in P.E. and Mr. Francis's Music Stars. New things mattered this year, like who had the coolest sneakers or whose paintings the teacher hung on the filing cabinet.

New things mattered, like who was who. And Room 19 was full of characters. . . .

Like Mimi. One time she stole a piece of printer paper when nobody was looking and called it a fluffy-wuffy bunny lost in a snowstorm. She had seen the actual *Mona Lisa* all the way across the ocean in France, so she called herself an *arteest*.

Is that what *arteests* do? It seemed like cheating to Audrey. It was just a piece of paper.

But Ms. Fincastle oohed and ahhed and asked Mimi to autograph it and then she hung it right at the tip-tip-top of her filing cabinet with three magnets shaped like little frogs.

And whose drawing was somewhere in the middle?

Dangling from one plain silver magnet?

Audrey's.

It was a rainbow made of only pink and purple and blue, with one cloud on either side. But each cloud was actually a face—Ms. Fincastle on one side, Audrey on the other.

Mimi had said those clouds made NO SENSE and were ALL WRONG and Audrey must never have paid attention in science because rainbows don't look like that.

Ms. Fincastle had called it *stupendous* and said Audrey was *a true creative talent*.

Except she still hung it underneath Mimi's.

So Mimi was the best at being an *arteest*.

Bettina was the best at putting up with Mimi. She'd listen when Mimi bossed her around and told her where to sit and when to stand and what to do.

Mimi and Bettina *together* made the best friendship bracelets. They'd never shared with Audrey.

Lena was the best at braids and taking care of the library basket.

Sonya ran faster than the third graders.

Von never got anything wrong on a spelling test. Not even the bonus words, the ones with four whole syllables.

And then there was Diego.

Diego had been Audrey's very first friend on the very first day of first grade, when he'd told her a knock-knock joke that made her laugh so hard, chocolate milk squirted out of her nose. He wasn't even grossed out, not one little bit.

Back then, Diego was the best at being a friend.

But this year, Diego and Kadir and Henley started the Acorn Club, which made Ms. Fincastle think they were being "responsible scientists," but really it was a joke-writing club that they had to keep a secret from Ms. Fincastle because sometimes their jokes were *inappropriate.*

The Acorn Club was truly the best at being funny. Diego must have forgotten that it was Audrey who had taught him all the best knock-knock jokes in first grade. And this year, when Diego told a knock-knock joke at lunch that made Audrey laugh so hard chocolate milk squirted out of her nose, he called her *Slimy Snot*. Kadir and Henley laughed and laughed and laughed.

He was definitely *not* the best at being a friend anymore.

Audrey was okay at braids and spelling and running (when she wasn't wearing sandals), but without Diego, she wasn't even sure she had a friend to practice being the best *to*.

Second grade was not twice as fun as first grade. It was way, way worse.

CHAPTER 2

"Little chickens!" said Ms. Fincastle.

Ms. Fincastle must have wanted to be a farmer before she became a teacher. She was always calling her students ducklings, or tiny piglets, or kids.

Audrey thought *kids* was extra funny because it meant child *and* baby goat. She wanted to let Ms. Fincastle know that she knew about that. Ms. Fincastle always got an eye twinkle when kids made a connection all on their very own. Did anybody else in Room 19 ever notice her eye twinkle?

Nope.

Nobody else noticed the sneakers in Ms. Fincastle's tote bag every Tuesday and Thursday, probably for dance class or something. Nobody else noticed that she only drank her coffee iced. Goldie had given her a Happy Birthday mug, but Ms. Fincastle used it for the dull pencils. She never ever, ever drank hot coffee.

Was Audrey the best at loving Ms. Fincastle?

"Want a hint about our Science Surprise Day creature? Only one week of waiting left!"

Science Surprise Day was definitely going to be one of the best parts of second grade. That was the day when Room 19 would get its first *actual living breathing* animal. Ms. Fincastle had been giving hints for weeks and weeks, which was one of those sneaky things teachers did to make kids pumped up for learning.

"Have you seen my glasses, wee ducklings?" Ms. Fincastle pat-pat-patted her head for her glasses, but they were already perched on the tip of her nose.

"THEY'RE ON YOUR FACE!" Room 19 yelled.

That was probably another teacher trick to make everyone comfortable and happy and ready to learn.

"Okey-dokey, settle down. We can't be *that* noisy because our creature for Science Surprise Day is *nocturnal*. That's when you sleep during the day and party all night."

"Oooh," said Bettina. "I hope it's a raccoon!"

"Bettina, honey," said Ms. Fincastle. "It is definitely *not* a raccoon. Now, do you want the good news or the bad news first?"

"BAAAAAAD!" Room 19 begged, all together.

"Okay," Ms. Fincastle said. "The bad news is that even though our creature is nocturnal, we will *not* be having a Room Nineteen sleepover."

"AWWWWWW," Room 19 said, all together.

Audrey hadn't ever thought about a sleepover at school, and now it sounded like the best thing ever. She could wear the slippers that Diego had given her for her birthday. They were fuzzy and yellow and shaped like bananas. Diego knew she'd love them. He said his mom had picked plain ones at first but he fixed that problem right up.

That was last year.

"But here's the good news!" Ms. Fincastle smushed her hands up under her chin.

"We have a brand-new owlet coming to Room Nineteen for good on Monday!"

"WHOOOO?" yelled Diego. He always made the funniest jokes.

"I'm so glad you asked, Diego," said Ms. Fincastle.

"Ms. Fincastle, do you mean a new student or another nocturnal creature?" Bettina asked.

"Ahh," said Ms. Fincastle. "A new *student* is joining us in Room Nineteen, and it's *still* not a raccoon."

A new student. Not a raccoon.

Audrey's belly did a floopity-flop deep, deep down.

"I want to tell you a little about her so that you will be welcoming, and helpful, and good citizens of Room Nineteen." Ms. Fincastle danced around the room.

The last time Audrey had gotten a real across-the-street new neighbor, it was Henley. His family moved into the house that used to be where seventeen cats lived. Mom always said there was no litter box big enough for seventeen cats, so maybe Audrey couldn't be *too* sure about all seventeen, but there were definitely *a lot* of cats living in that house. Most of them were gray and stripy and fuzzy, so it *could* have been the same cat over and over seventeen times. Still, Audrey liked to think she'd had seventeen cats for neighbors.

But when Henley moved in, the cats disappeared. Henley had four brothers, and they all made a bunch of noise. Their dad built a treehouse in the backyard that even had a swing! Diego came over all the time. Audrey wasn't allowed up.

So Audrey was cautious when it came to new neighbors. But if Ms. Fincastle was looking for somebody to be extra welcoming, Audrey was ready to try. She'd be the best citizen ever.

"Our new chickadee's favorite subjects in school are spelling and science and math and reading and writing." Ms. Fincastle paused for a moment of dramatic effect. "Her favorite thing to do is dance, and her very favorite snack is . . . chocolate-covered crickets."

"Chocolate-covered crickets?" said Bettina and Goldie and Sage all at once.

"Yep," said Ms. Fincastle. "I told you she liked science! She wrote a whole poem about her favorite insect unit at her old school."

"Can we do an insect unit and eat chocolate-covered crickets, Ms. Fincastle?" Diego was pumped up for learning.

See? It was working.

Would Ms. Fincastle put a poem about chocolate-covered crickets at the top of her filing cabinet?

"She'll join the Beluga Whales, since they've got an extra chair." Ms. Fincastle walked over to the table Audrey shared with Diego and Henley. Each table in Room 19 was named after one of the whale species they'd been studying in science. Diego and Henley were mad they weren't the Killer Whales, but Audrey loved how the word *beluuuuga* sounded.

"And Audrey L, I'd like you to be her Welcome Ambassador," continued Ms. Fincastle. "Because you have one particular thing in common—"

Wait.

Audrey *L*?

There had been a Charlie *M* and a Charlie *R* in kindergarten, but then they got split up in first grade because how is it fair to not just be who you are?

"That's right, little chickens. We have a brand-new Audrey!"

Until today, Audrey Locke was at least the best *Audrey* in Room 19.

And then Audrey Waters showed up.

CHAPTER 3

School was terrible.

Dinner was terrible.

Everything was terrible, but at least it was the weekend.

So Audrey and her mom and her little brother Bobo baked a cake.

Mom was truly the best at cakes. That's what happens when you are the head baker at a place called Cakes and Cakes and Cakes.

Dad was the best at eating them.

"I love your cakes and cakes and cakes and cakes and cakes and cakes and cakes," he'd always say, patting his belly, pretending to be full.

As for Bobo, he was the best at banging pots and pans. He was already an expert at steady beats. Audrey liked to tell him, *"Pianissimo, maestro!"* Everyone learned in kindergarten from Mr. Francis, the music teacher, that *pianissimo* was a fancy way to shush somebody *and* that it was very, very, very fun to say.

But today Bobo's clatter matched Audrey's insides, all jangly and rattly and antsy.

Audrey was pretty good at cakes. She was somewhere in between being the best at making them and the best at eating them. But when second grade squashes your dreams, even sweet vanilla frosting tastes sour.

"What if she wants five dollars to be her friend? What if she's invited to join the Acorn Club? What if she can sing 'The Star-Spangled Banner' backward?" Audrey scraped the bottom of the bowl with a spatula.

She didn't even feel like licking it. "Audrey L? I'm supposed to be just plain Audrey."

When Audrey smacked her fist down on the counter, flour poofed up and a fork clang-a-langed to the floor. Bobo laughed and stuck a chocolate chip up his nose.

"Well," Mom said, stirring golden batter with one hand and pinching Bobo's sugar-booger out with the other. "Think about how it might feel to be new and not have a friend yet. You wouldn't even know what day you can get chocolate milk! Now please pick up your fork."

Audrey thought about it.

She thought and she thought and she picked up her fork. Ms. Fincastle said this *new* Audrey loved chocolate-covered crickets. Audrey was definitely sure that this *new* Audrey wouldn't squirt chocolate milk out of her nose.

"But! There are sixteen other kids in Room Nineteen," she said. "Why do I have to be her Welcome Ambassador? It was my month to be On Vacation! That's the best job of all of them. Is it just because I'm an Audrey? What if she doesn't like me?"

Mom framed Audrey's cheeks with two sticky pinkies. She was sweet in the smile but salty in her eyes. "What if she does?"

Audrey thought. It would be nice to have a partner at the table. And Audrey was way more friend-ish than Diego and Henley these days. They probably wouldn't be very welcoming.

Right then and there, Audrey decided for sure: she would be the best Welcome Ambassador ever.

Mom twisted the kitchen timer and spun around so fast her apron strings twirled. "What do you think about the frosting? Vanilla? Cream cheese? Peanut butter?"

"Only grownups like cream cheese, Mom," Audrey said. "Let's do chocolate. I think this *new* Audrey would like that the most."

Yes, Audrey would be the best Welcome Ambassador she could be. And maybe, just maybe, this new Audrey would be like the old Diego.

CHAPTER 4

After the cake was all baked and sprinkled and tucked away from Dad and Bobo, Audrey opened her most favorite, favorite, favorite stationery set, the one she'd saved up for all by herself. It unfolded three times, with special spots for a notepad, four paisley-pastel-y pencils, some stickers, and a silver gelly pen. It was way better than spending money on Henley's tree-house password.

The stickers were half gone-and-stuck because Bobo had found them once and Audrey hadn't even gotten grumpy, because stickers are quieter than pots and pans. He didn't have to yell to stick some stickers.

What she loved most was the notepad.

Each note had her name at the top in big, blocky letters and purple glitter like this:

AUDREY

The bottom of each page had one of these four adorable things on it:

1. minty-green swoopy scoops of ice cream on a waffle cone

2. roller skates with flames flying out of the wheels

3. a fried egg with a smiley face in the yellowy yolk

4. AN ALICORN

Not many people know about alicorns. That's what you are when you are a unicorn with wings. Audrey tore off the top sheet, the swoopy scoops, and the next, the skates, and she stuck those underneath the stack at the bottom.

Audrey W might turn out to be like Mimi, or Diego, or Bobo. There was no way to tell yet.

The fried egg was the weirdest one. So that was the best one for Audrey W.

Audrey L sharpened a pencil, focused on her very best handwriting, and wrote a welcome.

Dear Audrey W,

Ms. Fincastle asked me to be your Welcome Ambassador.

So, welcome to Room 19 and the Beluga Whale table. We had an extra chair.

It's not covered in chocolate-covered crickets, but I still think you will like this cake.

From,
Audrey L

PS: I made sure Bobo's booger-hands didn't touch it. Do you have a brother? They are pretty gross.

She added the L at the last possible second.

CHAPTER 5

Dad drove Audrey to school early on Monday morning to make sure they didn't get stuck behind the trash truck. He and Mom were on the same team. They both said that a Welcome Ambassador needs to make their very best impression, and that meant not being late! Audrey took *s l o w* steps down the way-too-quiet, way-too-long hall, all the way down to Room 19. She was *s l o w* partly because she was careful to hold the cake plate with two hands and partly because she had mixed feelings about this *new* Audrey.

Audrey could feel her socks slipping lower and lower and lower, matching her mood. A small piece of her secretly hoped some of Bobo's boogers were baked inside.

Finally, she walked into Room 19.

"Good morning, Audrey Locke, my little lamb!" Ms. Fincastle must have gotten up with all of the sunshine and the *cock-a-doodle* rooster.

But Audrey L had definitely not, which was why she jumped, forgetting what was in her arms. At the exact time the cake hit the floor, a stranger walked in.

"Oh, fizzle-splits," said Audrey L, whispery like cotton candy.

And then Audrey L and Audrey W saw each other for the first time.

They were two strangers with *one particular thing* in common. Neither one said hello.

"Whoopsie!" Ms. Fincastle shimmied between the Audreys and scooped up the cake.

It had fallen like a kitty-cat, right side up but a little lopsided. It would have been *perfect* if Audrey L had been trying to make a pile of alicorn poop.

Audrey L's stomach hadn't felt this woozy since she'd accidentally swallowed her loose tooth in first grade. Back then, Diego had helped her write a letter to the Tooth Fairy explaining the situation, but she was all on her own now.

Audrey W looked at where the cake had fallen on the floor, and then at Audrey L. She couldn't take a step forward or else her spotless first-day shoes would have stepped right into the globs of frosting Ms. Fincastle was wiping up.

Audrey W was stuck. Would she laugh?

If Audrey W laughed at her, Audrey L would feel as lost as a fluffy-wuffy bunny in a snowstorm. But

Audrey W didn't laugh. She just stepped around the slippery spots and right to Ms. Fincastle's side.

Audrey L took a deep breath. "Welcome to Room Nineteen," she said, and handed her the welcome note. "I'm Audrey."

And then, somehow, Audrey W smiled and said, "I have this same stationery at home—it's my favorite."

CHAPTER 6

In all of the cake commotion, Audrey L must have stepped in some of that alicorn poop, because she was tromping a mess all over the floor of Room 19.

Ms. Fincastle *strongly suggested* Audrey L go clean up in the bathroom.

"Audrey W can join in with Diego and Henley for Morning Meeting," Ms. Fincastle told her. "Scoot."

Being warm and welcoming came easy to Diego, most of the time. And he definitely wouldn't throw a cake at the new Audrey. What if Diego was the best Welcome Ambassador? He didn't need to steal *two* new friends, right? He already had Henley.

Audrey L hopped down the long hall, skipping over the pea-green tiles, trying not to tromp any more of a mess. She didn't want Ms. Fincastle to get in trouble with the principal for having a wild child in Room 19.

But the hall was empty and quiet, and when nobody else was in the bathroom either, Audrey L yelled, *"CHOCOLATE-COVERED CRICKETS!"*

She liked the sound and the dizzy-dazzle scramble of the echo. It rattled off the walls and felt a little dangerous.

She stretched up her leg and propped her foot on the sink. Then she soaked and rubbed and wiped down her shoes. She heard Ms. Fincastle in her head, asking if she was a *responsible scientist*, and thought that she'd probably wasted too many paper towels.

On the way back to Room 19, Audrey L thought about the things she had in common with Audrey W. They had the same name. They had the same teacher. They had the same stationery.

But Audrey L had already seen one major differ-
ence between them: Audrey W's first-day shoes.
They were the coolest sneakers. They had bright
ink splotches dotted along the edges—the kind of
splotches that were supposed to be there, not blobs

of paint she'd dripped on accident. The splotches were so colorful that you could wear any outfit you wanted with them and they would *still* match. Audrey L had wanted that exact pair, but she still fit into her last-day-of-first-grade shoes, so Mom said no. Instead, Audrey L had made her own splotches when she got bored of singing and colored her shoes with marker in Mr. Francis's class.

It was not the same.

It took sixteen paper towels to get as close as she could to Audrey W's brand-new first-day shoes. But hers were still handmade and greasy.

As she walked back to Room 19, Audrey L thought about some more differences she already knew about.

Audrey W wrote poems for fun!

Audrey L had to work super-duper-duper hard to be only okay at spelling.

Audrey W liked to dance!

Audrey L twisted her ankle when she tripped over Dad's garden hose.

Audrey W could probably even say "A baboon's balloon flew up to the moon" eight times fast without messing up.

". . . babloon-balloon-floogle-guppy-blue-moon."

"Audrey L?"

As soon as her tongue had been properly twisted, Audrey L realized thirty-six eyes were staring up at her from the reading rug in Room 19. And there she was, babbling on about baboons.

CHAPTER 7

The rest of the morning went okay.

"Did you get all the goo off your shoes?" Audrey W asked Audrey L, when all of Room 19 had left the rug and were shuffling back to their tables. "I mean, not goo like gross. Goo like . . ."

"Goo! It was definitely goo. Delicious goo, but goo," Audrey L said.

Audrey L didn't know if it was weird to talk about goo with somebody right after you'd met them. It wasn't really a get-to-know-you question, like *What's your favorite color?* or *Do you like roller coasters?* or *Would you rather have an alien or an otter for a pet?*

"Goo is my favorite dessert," said Audrey W.

"Which is better—Marshmallow Fluff or raspberry ice cream?" Audrey L asked.

"Marshmallow Fluff," said Audrey W. "Obviously."

"Marshmallow Fluff or chocolate-covered crickets?" Audrey L asked again.

"Chocolate-covered crickets!" Diego laughed and laughed—as if Audrey L had even been asking him.

Audrey W looked like she wanted to hide under the table.

"Diego," said Audrey L. "Remember when you ate a crayon to see if you could color with your fingernails?"

And that was that. The Beluga Whales got back to work.

"Thank you," Audrey W whispered.

After social studies and a snack and a sixty-second cleanup, Ms. Fincastle dinged her cheery chime and sent Room 19 off to music class.

Mr. Francis's music room was in the basement. It took thirteen steps to get all the way down. That's how Audrey L had known since kindergarten that the letter *M* was smack-dab in the middle of the alphabet. She'd sing reallllly quietly on the way down to get her voice box juiced up and ready. She'd get all the way to *M* on the way to music, and after, she'd start at *N* and go all the way back up the steps to *Z*.

The only bad thing about the music room was that it didn't have any windows. There was carpet on the walls and faded bulletin boards that hadn't been changed in forever, unless the trombone had been the INSTRUMENT OF THE WEEK for eighty-seven weeks. It was like whoever built the school knew that music class would be so loud and rowdy, it needed to be stuffed downstairs. Still, it didn't seem fair to leave Mr. Francis without some fresh air.

The second everyone had trickled into Mr. Francis's room, Mimi grabbed Audrey W by the hand like she was a puppy on a leash and pulled her over to Mr. Francis. Audrey L should have been the one to introduce her, but she was still thinking about that trombone.

"Mr. Francis, did you hear about the other Audrey?"

"What Audrey?" Mr. Francis asked. He obviously wasn't expecting a new Audrey, and it seemed like he'd forgotten the old one! Audrey L felt invisible. He *did* teach hundreds of musicians, but was it too much to ask that her own music teacher know who she was?

"We got a new Audrey! So now there's two—like Charlie M and Charlie R," Mimi said. "Audrey L hasn't been a Music Star yet, so it's not like you have to fix her name or anything." Mimi had been the very first Music Star of the second grade, and she never let anyone forget it.

"Ahh, Audrey, yes," Mr. Francis's eyes scanned the room and landed on Isabella.

"No, *I'm* Audrey," both Audreys said. They looked at each other.

"Jinx." Audrey W took one step away from Mimi and one step closer to Audrey L.

Thankfully, Mr. Francis ignored Mimi and shook Audrey W's hand instead. And then he sat down at the piano, plunked out a scale, and Room 19 sang *baa baa baa baa bum* up and down until they were all warmed up.

The Acorn Club liked the *bum* part.

Then Mr. Francis explained the rules to a brand-new activity. It was called Instrument Twin, and everyone got a piece of paper with an instrument on it. The instruments were all things Mr. Francis had in the music room— ukuleles, triangles, sand blocks, the djembe drums, maracas. Two people had the same instrument on their papers, and you'd have to walk around and sing the sound your instrument makes to find your Instrument Twin. Once you found your match, you could play beats or scales from the basket at each station. Or you could even make up your own song.

Usually, Room 19 had an odd number of kids, which meant one pair had to become a trio, a twosome with an extra someone. This year, that someone had always been Audrey, always left over. Now that Audrey W was here, there was zilch, zero, *no way* she'd be left over. Audrey L wouldn't let that happen. She was much too welcoming for that.

Soon the room filled up with pa-ta-slaps and doop-doop-doos and plingy-bongs.

Diego and Goldie paired up with a fhh-shh-shh.

Audrey looked at her paper. She wished super hard that Audrey W would be a glockenspiel too.

Lena thunked and Henley thudded together.

Audrey L wished harder.

Mimi was a bow-wow-wow sound, which meant she *definitely* wasn't a glockenspiel.

Clumps of partners dotted the room, and finally Audrey L heard it.

A TING! A TANG! A glockenspiel!

Audrey L couldn't believe her luck. Audrey W WAS a glockenspiel too! This was the best day.

"Mr. Francis is kinda funny, right?" Audrey W whispered.

"Yeah!" said Audrey L. "I think it's the fourth graders' fault that he's a little scatterbrained. They play the recorders, but they are *not* true creative talents."

"What do you mean?" asked Audrey W.

"Oh," said Audrey L. "They are awful. Super screechy. I'd probably teach them egg shakers instead and save my eardrums."

Audrey L felt a little bad for making fun of the fourth graders, even though it was true. But she felt as important as the trombone when Audrey W smiled again.

"What about the glockenspiel?" Audrey W handed Audrey L a mallet.

But before they could even bang one bar, the fire alarm went off. It was loud and rattly and the light was flickery and it was so startling that someone shrieked.

Someone always shrieked in the fire drills.

"I know it hurts our ears, but it's loud to keep us safe! Aren't we glad we hear it and can see the flashing lights?" Mr. Francis grabbed his clipboard. "*A-B-C* order, maestros!"

Now Audrey W looked lost. Ms. Fincastle's room wasn't organized by *A-B-C* order. And she didn't know everyone's names yet!

"Here, come with me," Audrey L said.

"Okay," said Audrey W.

But as they headed out the door, single file and straight past Mr. Francis, he said, "*A-B-C* order is for *last* names, girls. Audrey W, you're almost the caboose. Right in front of Bettina, okay?"

"Okay," said Audrey W, and she waited for the end of the line to file past.

"But, Mr. Francis, I'm her Welcome Ambassador! She doesn't know where to fit in yet." Audrey L kept her

place in between Henley and Sonya but yelled behind her so Mr. Francis would hear over the fire alarm.

"Walk quickly, and please stop talking!"

Room 19 marched all the way outside to the gathering spot on the lawn, still lined up in *A-B-C* order. Mr. Francis patted each of them on the head and put checkmarks on his clipboard to be sure they were all still together.

"Mr. Francis! I didn't mean to bring out this ukulele!" Wesley held up a bright orange one over his head.

"Wesley, shhh! No talking, please. Just hold it, okay?"

Audrey L peeked toward the back of the line.

Bettina and Audrey W were not following the fire-drill rules.

They were chitchatting, and every once in a while, one of them would giggle. Every time Mr. Francis walked closer to that end of the line, they'd get as quiet as fluffy-wuffy bunnies. And every time he turned around again, they'd get right back to giggling.

It had felt so nice to be a glockenspiel with Audrey W.

But maybe Bettina was the one who would be her first real friend in Room 19.

Audrey L and Audrey W hadn't had a laugh together yet. She still didn't know if Audrey W would rather have an alien or an otter for a pet. They'd been glockenspiels for barely one ding.

Audrey L usually loved fire drills because you got to leave a mess behind and nobody asked you to clean it up. But today, she'd rather sharpen every single pencil in the second grade.

CHAPTER 8

Mom and Dad and Bobo and Audrey went out for pizza that night. They always did on Mondays. It was a family tradition.

Pizza Bernal was kitty-corner from Cakes and Cakes and Cakes, and so of course Dad made his favorite joke about how Pizza Bernal should be called Pies and Pies and Pies.

Dad swore that some people called pizza *pizza pie*, but that made zero sense to Audrey. Pies have fillings, not toppings. And anyway, the only person who ever laughed at that joke was Diego. Diego Bernal. It was his parents' pizza place.

Sometimes Diego gave menus and crayons to little kids, but most of the time he sat at a corner booth drawing comics and reading joke books.

So every time the Locke family went to Pizza Bernal, Dad invited Diego to join them. Mom liked that Diego would eat the green pepper side with Dad, and Bobo liked to pretend he had a brother.

It was fine in first grade, but now? Eating dinner every week with Diego was *not* Audrey's favorite thing. It probably wasn't Diego's favorite either. It was a reminder every single week that they used to have things to talk about, like whether spiders or scorpions were scarier or how many more sequins could fit on the principal's jean jacket—Mrs. Louis *loved* sequins.

But now, they barely even talked at all.

"How was school?" Dad wiggled out an oozy-gooey-cheesy piece of pizza.

"Do you mean besides the whole *alicorn poop* thing?" Diego said.

Bobo laughed and laughed and laughed like he had never heard the word *poop* before.

Mom wrapped an arm around Audrey and pulled her close on the girls' side of the booth. But when Audrey scooted over, the booth made a fruppity-fizz sound. That made Diego and even Dad laugh along with Bobo. Audrey could not imagine anything worse.

Mom gave them all a look that said *Stop it and snap out of it,* and at least Diego did.

"It was great, right, Audrey?" said Diego. "Ms. Fincastle kept forgetting where her glasses were, and the other Audrey came, and we had a fire drill in music class, and later Wesley broke a string on his ukulele and pretended it was dental floss, but then his actual tooth came out and Mr. Francis almost fainted."

It was all true.

Wesley was definitely *not* a Music Star that week.

"And did you hear how Audrey stood in front of the whole class and told everyone everything she knows about baboons?"

"Diego!" said Audrey. She wanted to fly away.

"Baboons?" Mom asked, her arm wrapping tighter.

"Yeah," said Diego.

Audrey sank as low as she could go while still keeping her bum on the booth. That was Mom's rule, and it was usually directed at Bobo.

"What does a baboon like to play with?" Dad wiped pizza grease on his napkin, eyes sparkling, like he had spent the afternoon reading Diego's joke books.

Diego knew it. "Bab-*boomerangs!*"

"What do you call a mischief-making monkey?"

"A *bad*-boon!"

"What is a baboon's favorite cookie?"

"Chocolate chimp!"

Maybe because it was about a delicious dessert, or maybe because she forgot about the scooching sound and the way everyone had laughed at Audrey, but the worst sound in the world was when *Mom* started laughing along with everyone else.

Forget being the best.

Audrey wasn't even any good at pizza night with her very own family.

CHAPTER 9

Tuesday was new. Anything could happen on a Tuesday.

At the clang of Ms. Fincastle's chimes, Room 19 speed-walked to the hall. Every single second of recess was important. That was when most of the friend-ish stuff happened. That's when Mimi and Bettina made their friendship bracelets. It was when the Acorn Club held their top-secret meetings. It was when Goldie and Sage Hula-Hooped for thirteen minutes and sixteen seconds in a row. They'd only made it to nine and a half minutes in first grade.

Everyone gathered at their cubbies first—they had to get their snacks and fill up their water bottles.

And somehow—*magically* somehow—Audrey L and Audrey W's cubbies were side by side.

They'd also both worn sandals, and they both had nail polish on their toes—the purple kind, just like the color of the AUDREY on their notepads. What were the chances?

"Blueberry Smash?" Audrey W asked.

"Very Violet," said Audrey L.

"I love it," said Audrey W.

"I love yours too," said Audrey L.

Audrey W's nail polish was sparkly and Audrey L's was not. And Bobo had thought her pinky toe was a jellybean and grabbed it with his pudgy thumbs, so it was smudged. But other than that, the two Audreys' toes looked mostly the same.

Both sandals, both purples. Was that friend-ish?

"Do you want to race to the top of the climber? You can see the teacher parking lot from the top. Coach

Mallory hasn't cleaned the bird poop off his truck in seven weeks," said Audrey L.

"Gross!" said Audrey W.

"I know!" said Audrey L.

The girls reached the climber at almost the same exact time, but there was a problem. Mrs. Wilson, the teacher on Yard Duty, gave them a big fat NO because they were wearing sandals and it was *dangerous*.

"PLEASE," Audrey L begged.

"Laces only. Sorry, friend," Mrs. Wilson said. Was Mrs. Wilson their friend? Audrey L didn't think so.

At the same exact time, they both said, "Fine—we'll swing!"

And at the same exact time, they both said, "JINX!" Again.

"We can do the climber on Friday. Wear sneakers, okay?" Audrey L said.

"Deal," said Audrey W.

"Ms. Fincastle has Yard Duty on Fridays. You know how you usually need three people for double Dutch? Well, sometimes she'll tie the ends of two jump ropes to the climber and spin the others for me. Then we switch and she'll jump too! She's not very good, but she reallllly loves it."

"Ms. Fincastle plays with you?" asked Audrey W.

"Sometimes she even lets me fling around her whistle and pretend to lasso Diego with it. I'm just not allowed to put my own spit on it."

"Yeah, that does seem like a pretty good idea," said Audrey W.

Recess had barely started, but it was the first recess Audrey could remember having fun at. In fact, it was the first day all year that Audrey L hadn't asked whoever was on Yard Duty how many more minutes were left. Even just wandering around with somebody else was better than pretending she *wanted* to double Dutch with Ms. Fincastle. Audrey L loved Ms. Fincastle, but most of the time she was the only one to play with. It was a little embarrassing, even if nobody else even seemed to notice.

"Did you ever play Washing Machine at your old school?" Audrey L put her belly across the swing.

She was careful to keep her hair and fingers out of the chains. One time Diego had a little problem with the chains and his pinky finger and so he spent all of lunchtime in the sickroom. Audrey L could still picture the gross Band-Aid he wore for one whole week. Diego said that was because it had Thor on it and he didn't want to throw his superpowers out with the trash.

"What's Washing Machine?" Audrey W asked, matching Audrey L's belly-to-swing pose.

"Okay, so do this." Audrey L dug her toes into the dirt.

When she turned, the swing creaked.

When she twirled, the swing screeched.

And when she twisted, it squeeeeeeaked.

After Audrey L was all wound up tight—she let go.

"WAAAAAAASSSSSSSSSHHHHHHHHIIING
MAAAACHHHHHHIIIIINE!!"

The twirls became wails and the squeaks became
squeals and both girls spun and spun and squawked
and spun.

"That was awesome," Audrey W said breathlessly.

"I'm so glad I didn't wear laces, *friend*." Audrey L imitated the way Mrs. Wilson had said it.

"Same here, *friend*." Audrey W did too.

And they both laughed.

CHAPTER 10

By the time Audrey L got home, she was pooped. All she wanted to do was collapse onto the couch or practice crisscross jump rope. But when she walked into the living room, something was very unusual. She was looking right at Bobo's hind parts. "Bobo?" Audrey crouched down next to him.

"I can't find Red," Bobo said, a little muffled. Audrey had given Bobo a fire truck for his third birthday. *Red*, he'd named it. But Red had come with batteries and was as loud as Bobo, which meant that sometimes Dad hid it in the coat closet.

"Okay, but why are you halfway under the couch?"

Bobo squiggled himself backward like a snake with a belly tickle.

"Audrey, this is the parking garage," Bobo said, like it was something everybody knew. Like how blue and yellow make green, or how Pizza Bernal didn't serve mushrooms because Mr. Bernal was allergic to them. Although maybe Audrey was the only one who had ever noticed that.

"Right, right." Audrey plopped herself onto the middle cushion. She knew Bobo would be close behind. "What if we park everything else first? Maybe Red will drive up later?"

Bobo would wear his pajamas inside out if Audrey suggested it. He lined up all of his cars and then slithered up onto the couch with her.

It was a good, sweet, snuggly plan. Audrey waited through half of Bobo's favorite show. Then she moved his small hand from her knee and tried her best to wriggle away secretly.

Audrey was successful.

She made it to the coat closet. She was right.

Then she wriggled back, parked Red right near the entrance to the parking garage, and slunk back up onto the couch. All before Bobo budged.

Audrey waited one whole minute. Then she said, "Bobo!" and pointed.

Bobo's whole body turned into a grin. He scooped up Red, stuck him in between the two of them, and they all finished watching the show together.

CHAPTER 11

Wednesdays were for spelling tests.

Audrey L was not *stupendous* at spelling, so Wednesdays were also for being super-duper-duper nervous.

"Paper-Passer-Outers!" Ms. Fincastle nodded to Bettina and Von, who got to work.

"Here you go, new Audrey and old Audrey," said Bettina, dropping a pile of spelling-test papers on their table. She wasn't very careful about it, so most of them slid right to the floor.

"Come on, Bettina. Don't be rude." Diego scooped up the papers and handed one each to Audrey L, Audrey W, and Henley.

"Thanks, Diego," said Audrey L.

"Beluga Whales stick together," said Diego. "It's called a *pod*."

Diego could definitely be nice some of the time. Audrey L missed when it was all of the time.

Von came by with the Secret Shields. He gave the Belugas two yellows, one purple, and one green. Audrey L snagged the purple one before the boys could, and gave it to Audrey W.

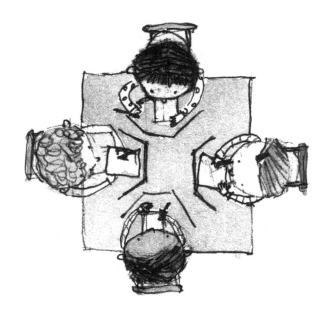

Audrey W peeked around her Secret Shield sneaky-quick. "Did you study?"

"*Y-E-S*," Audrey L said.

It was a little bit true, but Audrey L had gotten stuck in Bobo's parking lot the night before for a long, long time. So since it didn't hurt to wish for luck, she crisscrossed the fingers on her left hand and blew the silver sparkles off the tip-top of the pencil.

The spelling list was tricky and very *mix-up-able*. It was all homophones, those funny words that sound the same but mean something totally completely definitely different—like how someone would say, *Smell this flower, isn't it nice?* instead of *Smell this flour, isn't it nice?*

Audrey L was as ready as she could be.

"The first word is *bear*. I was really hoping to eat that chicken salad sandwich, but a *bear* stole my picnic basket. *Bear*."

Ms. Fincastle was the best at making spelling tests great. (Not *grate*.) She could even make chicken salad sandwiches sound delicious.

Twenty words later, the test was over. Bettina and Von came back around for the spelling tests and Secret Shields, and Audrey L whooshed out a deep breath of happiness. She was pretty sure Audrey W did too.

Before Ms. Fincastle let them loose for P.E., she gave them one more Science Surprise Day hint.

"On Science Surprise Day this Friday, you will *S-E-E* something that comes from the *S-E-A*. But they can live in both land and sea. Ours will be a landlubber—that means someone who lives on land—because Room Nineteen doesn't have an ocean." Ms. Fincastle winked one eye extra tight, which made a bunch of crinkles in the corners. "Now get out of here. And no running on the way to P.E.—conserve that energy for Coach Mallory, please!"

Ms. Fincastle trusted the second graders to get themselves to P.E. on their own, because all they had to do was slip out the double doors and they were thirty-eight steps from the gym. Most of Room 19 ignored Ms. Fincastle about running, but she never really fussed at them. *There are bigger fish to fry* is what Dad always said.

Audrey L figured she didn't fuss because P.E. was Ms. Fincastle's first break of the day. And she knew teachers deserved a break. When else would Ms. Fincastle finish her coffee? At least it was already icy cold.

While Mimi and Bettina and Goldie and the Acorn Club ran ahead, both Audreys walked.

Together.

"So what's this Science Surprise Day?" Audrey W asked.

"Oh!" said Audrey L. "You are going to love it. We heard all about how much you love science."

Audrey W bounced a little when Audrey L even said the WORD *science*.

"And you came to Room Nineteen just in time, because it's happening on Friday!"

"Really?" said Audrey W.

"Yeah! Ms. Fincastle's been sharing hints about this creature—you know, to get us pumped up for learning—and we've all been trying to figure out what it is," said Audrey L. "Do you want to know the rest of the hints?"

Audrey W bounced higher. "Of course!"

For a lickety-split second, Audrey L thought about making up some of the hints to stump Audrey W, but that was not very welcoming (or being a responsible scientist) so she told the truth.

Isn't that something friends would do?

"Well, it's got ten legs but could fit in a chocolate-milk carton," said Audrey L. "And Ms. Fincastle said 'Sometimes you see it, sometimes you don't.'"

"Hmm," said Audrey W. "And it's something aquatic, right? That's what Ms. Fincastle hinted this morning." Was something that comes from the *S-E-A* the same thing as *aquatic*? Audrey L didn't ask.

"One of the fourth graders said Ms. Fincastle brought in an alligator when they were in second grade, but I think that's against the law," said Audrey L.

"And an alligator definitely doesn't fit into a chocolate-milk carton," said Audrey W. "I think I know!"

"What about a *baby* alligator, though?" Audrey L loved guessing. She started to skip a little.

So did Audrey W.

"Speaking of chocolate-milk cartons," Audrey L said, "did anyone tell you Thursdays are Chocolate Milk Day in the cafeteria? And if you tell Mrs. Buzzard that her bun looks nice, she'll sometimes give you two." She paused. "Just be careful that you say *bun* and not *buns*. You know."

"Eww," Audrey W said. "Don't make me picture her *buns!*"

They screamed and ran all the way to the gym. And when they slowed down to go inside, Audrey W said, "Thanks, Audrey."

Just

plain

Audrey.

And she smiled.

CHAPTER 12

The gym looked weird. It wasn't set up for relay races or basketball.

There were big plastic balls sitting in big laundry bins lined along the floor. They were the kind of balls that Mom used for yoga and were strictly off-limits to Bobo.

Audrey L had never seen a scene like this before.

"Whoa," said Audrey W. "I've never seen a scene like this before."

Before Coach Mallory said anything, Audrey L and Audrey W picked two balls right next to each other. Audrey L stood by a gloomy gray one so that Audrey W could have the purple.

"Good morning, Team Fincastle," said Coach Mallory.

He wore sweatbands on his forehead and wrist and other wrist and each ankle. Audrey L wasn't too sure what kind of sweating your ankles were supposed to do in P.E., but then again, she wasn't the best athlete on Team Fincastle.

Besides, Coach Mallory was the boss.

"You have each chosen a—*drumroll, please*—"

Everyone in Room 19 did the only obvious thing to do—they rat-a-tat-tatted and bing-bong-banged their fingers and hands all over the yoga balls in baskets. It sounded like a rainstorm in a bounce house until Coach Mallory blew his whistle one-two-three times, *quick-quick-quick.*

"A drum. You've each chosen—a drum."

Diego was the only one who laughed.

"We are about to have a BLOOD! PUMPING! BONANZA! But first, you need to take the Pledge of the Drumsticks." There were buckets of drumsticks at the end of each line, and Coach Mallory lifted one high in the air and then spun it like he was a rock star.

Audrey L wanted to giggle and roll her eyes at Coach Mallory. She thought for sure Audrey W would too, but nope. She stood there like she was on a field trip to a museum—still and quiet and ready.

Audrey L snapped to attention. She didn't need to be the best, but she wanted to keep up. If Audrey W was way into this drumming thing, Audrey L would be too.

"Repeat after me, Team Fincastle," Coach Mallory said. "I promise!"

"I promise!"

"That I will use these drumsticks only on the drums!"

"That I will use these drumsticks only on the drums!"

"I will not use them—"

"I will not use them—"

"On someone I do not like or even a friend!"

"On someone I do not like or even a friend!"

"And that's because, Team Fincastle—"

"And that's because, Coach Mallory—"

"I like everyone anyway and I will use common sense with my drumsticks so I can feel the burn, HEY-HO!"

"I like everyone anyway and I will use common sense with my drumsticks so I can feel the burn, LET'S GO!"

Most of Room 19 got to the LET'S GO part. One of the boys said something like "Burn sense ba-da bumsticks," but it was close enough.

"Sticks up, Team Fincastle!" Coach Mallory held his drumsticks in an X over his head. "It's time for Team Fincastle's Drumstick Championship!" He was extremely serious about both common sense *and* feeling the burn.

Coach Mallory smacked his sticks together for eight counts, whacked the ball for eight counts, and then alternated back and forth. That part was easy. But then his patterns got quicker and quicker and harder to remember. Every once in a while, he'd even smack the basket itself.

So Team Fincastle repeated each series of drills and rhythms and rat-a-tat-tats as best they could. It challenged their muscles and their flexibility and their balance and their rhythm.

Fizzle-splits, thought Audrey L. She was really feeling the burn.

Audrey W was barely breaking a sweat.

One by one, Team Fincastle missed a beat or a bounce or a thump or a shake. And one by one, they set their drumsticks down.

First Wesley. Then Mimi.

Then Kadir, Sage, and Bettina.

Goldie. William. Diego.

Somewhere in the middle, Audrey L.

And then Jamie, Isabella, George, and Charlie.

Sonya. Von. Lena. Henley.

Audrey W was the last kid standing. She was the best—Team Fincastle's Drumstick Championship Champion.

No way she'd need a *somewhere in the middle* friend like Audrey L.

CHAPTER 13

Ms. Fincastle met her little chickens at the door of Room 19.

"Your spelling tests are graded and on your desks, people. Take a peek, but don't show a friend, okay? Your grade, your business."

There it was, Audrey L's test. It was graded in Ms. Fincastle's favorite purple pen.

And then! The best thing!

On top of Audrey L's paper was a stamp that said *YOU ROCK!* and Ms. Fincastle had added four extra exclamation marks in her purple pen!!!!

It was a perfect score, a *stupendous* score. She hugged the paper to her heart, which was now feeling the burn of happiness.

"Umm, Ms. Fincastle?" said Audrey W. "I think there's a teensy tiny mix-up."

Audrey L's heart fizzled. When she looked closer, she noticed that the *CK!* in *YOU ROCK!* covered up a W.

"Oopsy-daisy! Swap-a-roo, Audreys!"

When Audrey L got her *real* spelling test back, there was no *YOU ROCK!* Just a stamp with a snail saying, GOOD START, and zero exclamation marks.

She got three word pairs wrong, wrong, wrong.

Aisle and *isle*.

Flea and *flee*.

Heel and *heal*.

Audrey L was definitely only okay at spelling.

But then Audrey W made a heart with her fingers and whispered, *"You rock too."*

Nobody had ever told her that before besides Mom.

Audrey L felt like maybe—just maybe—something kind of friend-ish was better than four exclamation marks in Ms. Fincastle's favorite purple pen.

CHAPTER 14

It had been a really long week in Room 19.

The alicorn poop.

The fire drill.

Team Fincastle's Drumstick Championship.

The spelling test.

The friend-ish stuff.

But it was finally Friday, and that meant three of the very best things for Audrey L:

1. It was Ms. Fincastle's Yard Duty Day.

2. It was Science Surprise Day.

3. It was *almost* Saturday.

Maybe Audrey W was the best at drumming on yoga balls. Maybe she was also the best at spelling tricky homophones. But Audrey L was *definitely* the best at baking.

And Saturday was for baking with Audrey W.

Dad had a work meeting bright and early, which meant Audrey L got to Room 19 brighter and earlier. She helped Ms. Fincastle sort the colored pencils into rainbow order. She sharpened the dull pencils with the used-up erasers. She even scribbled with each marker to make sure they worked right. Not even Mimi deserved to do art with dried-up duds.

Once Room 19's supplies were all straightened out, Audrey L had an idea.

"Excuse me, Ms. Fincastle? Can I have a piece of paper from the printer?"

"Absolutely! Thank you for asking." Ms. Fincastle must have been remembering that time when Mimi did *not* ask.

Printer paper definitely wasn't the same as alicorn stationery.

But wasn't it also from the heart? Wouldn't that be special too?

Dear Audrey W,

I can't wait to bake with you!

Audrey L

When Audrey L finished her note, she folded it up and slid it into her back pocket, where all the most important things went.

Ms. Fincastle was still scribbling away at something of her own, so Audrey L sneak-tiptoed around in case the Science Surprise was hiding somewhere. But it was more like a squeak-tiptoe. Audrey L's shoes were too loud for sneaking around.

"All done?" Ms. Fincastle asked.

"Yep," said Audrey. "All done."

"Good. I've got something for you. Get over here, chickadee."

Sitting down, Ms. Fincastle was the same size as Audrey L. She looked straight into her eyes. "I goofed big-time yesterday with the spelling tests," she said.

"Yeah," said Audrey L.

"And I'm really sorry about that." Ms. Fincastle put a hand on one of Audrey L's, and even though it was iced-coffee cold, it felt warm and welcoming.

Audrey L didn't say anything. She wasn't sure it was okay yet.

"I don't know if *you* have a filing cabinet to hang your favorite things on, but I made this for you anyway."

It was a picture of Audrey L herself—she could tell by the hair and the purple shirt with an alicorn on it. And then, in all the wide-open space around her head, Ms. Fincastle had written words in bubbly rainbow letters. Words like STUPENDOUS!

RELIABLE! PERSISTENT! MAGNIFICENT! AMAZ-
ING! and WELCOME AMBASSADOR!

"You *more* than rock, Audrey," said Ms. Fincastle.

Audrey L hugged the drawing to her heart, just like
she had done with the spelling test.

"Thank you," she said, and she meant it.

And then Audrey L happily squeak-tiptoed around
the room again until Diego showed up.

Audrey L wasn't sure at first that it *was* Diego, because he was dressed up with googly eyes and some kind of claw thing. "What are you? An elf?" asked Audrey L.

"Audrey L," he said, "How can you not S-E-E that I am a hermit crab who comes from the S-E-A?" Then he pinched at her. Even though Audrey L was not afraid of kitchen tongs, she still flinched.

"I see *someone* must have spilled the beans about Science Surprise Day." Ms. Fincastle crossed her arms and looked like she'd stepped in alicorn poop.

"It's not my fault, Ms. Fincastle," said Diego. "I can't help it that some third graders ride the early bus."

Mmm-hmmm.

Diego was maybe not the Most Responsible Scientist.

But he was definitely a resourceful one.

CHAPTER 15

If it had been first grade, Diego might have told her that the secret creature coming on Science Surprise Day was a hermit crab so Audrey L could have *also* worn a red bike helmet and stuck kitchen tongs in her jacket.

But it wasn't first grade. Diego had the Acorn Club now and didn't need Audrey L at all.

But maybe she had someone new too?

Audrey L forgot about giving her printer-paper note to Audrey W. Now all she could think about was telling her about Science Surprise Day. Sharing a secret was definitely a friend-ish thing to do.

Audrey L waited next to the lockers until she saw

Audrey W, and then she ran up to her. Ms. Fincastle always said not to run, but this was important.

"Something *magnificent* is happening in science today. Look at Diego!"

Audrey L grabbed Audrey W's hand. They peeked into the classroom to watch Ms. Fincastle help Diego with his gear. She hung up his bike helmet and wrestled a little with the tongs, then stuck them on the hooks like they were a regular old rain jacket.

"Well," Audrey W said. "That's weird."

"Well," Audrey L said. "*He's* weird."

"Is he supposed to be an elf?" Audrey W mostly let go of Audrey L's hand, but she kept the pinky close, the way real friends do.

"That's what I thought too!" said Audrey L, and she squeezed Audrey W's pinky back.

"Come on in and gather around, you giggly goats!" Ms. Fincastle shepherded seventeen kids plus one halfway hermit crab onto the rug. "You might guess that Diego is celebrating bike safety week or working a shift at Cakes and Cakes and Cakes, but nope. He's just *stupendously spirited* for our Science Surprise Day visitor. *This* little guy!"

Ms. Fincastle reached into a brown paper bag, the crumply-crinkly kind you get at the grocery store with all the free samples on Saturdays. She pulled out a small plastic tank with a bright orange lid that almost looked empty. But snuggled in the middle of a pile of wood chips was a big brown swirly shell.

"This," said Ms. Fincastle, "is our newest student in Room 19."

Audrey L was full of alicorn sparkles for Audrey W because she wasn't the newest anymore. Audrey L turned to say, "You're not the newest anymore!"

But right then, Audrey W got something out of her pocket. "I brought breakfast!" she said. It was a plastic baggie, smushed full with sunflower seeds and blueberries and oats.

So she must have known who the Science Surprise Day visitor would be too.

But how?

She didn't ride the early bus, so no third graders had spilled the beans.

Had Ms. Fincastle told Audrey W the secret first?

No way. Was she just *so* smart and *so* good at spelling and science and BLOOD! PUMPING! BONANZAS! that she had just figured it out all on her own?

But sharing secrets was a perfectly friend-ish thing to do, right? Why hadn't Audrey W told her about it? Audrey L had plenty of oats at home that she could have dumped into a plastic baggie. Mom wouldn't even have missed them. Suddenly, Audrey L didn't care about the crab anymore. She didn't care about

Ms. Fincastle's drawing. She could only think about one thing.

Audrey L pictured the printer-paper note in her back pocket. In her imagination, she ripped the note to pieces and threw it away.

CHAPTER 16

Room 19 spent the first part of Science Surprise Day hypothesizing and observing and wondering about the thing in the big brown swirly shell. They watched videos and checked out library books and let it tickle-crawl all over their hands.

Ms. Fincastle taught them how hermit crabs eat and how they skitter-skatter. She taught them how *sometimes* crabs are friendly, but they also like alone time.

Audrey L could definitely relate to this hermit crab.

Then Ms. Fincastle said, "Our new friend can't go without a name, can she?"

And that's what made Audrey think things would turn back around.

Diego had worn a goofy outfit. Audrey W had brought the hermit crab some healthy treats. But this next part? Audrey L was ready to do something really special for Science Surprise Day too.

"And so, little chicks, we each need to brainstorm what to name our *fabulous-crabulous* friend."

Ms. Fincastle handed everyone a clump of sticky notes and told them to put their crab name ideas on the front of each sticky and their real name on the back, and then fold them and stick them to the board by the time lunch was over.

Audrey L could hardly eat her lunch, even though she always got to pack potato chips on Fridays. She was absolutely, positively, definitely a true creative talent and *way* ready for this.

AUDREY L's HERMIT CRAB NAME IDEAS

Bumbleberry

Pepperoni

Cadillac

Moonrock

Cha-Cha Domino

Pianissimo

Gertie

Bow-Tie Bob

Beluga

Bobo

Glockenspiel

CHAPTER 17

After lunch, Ms. Fincastle read *alllllllll* of the sticky notes while Room 19 got to read whatever they wanted. Audrey L grabbed one of the nonfiction books the librarian had delivered on Tuesday.

Except the first page she flipped to was a colorful

chart that said what hermit crabs eat. Audrey L closed it tight and kept her eyes on Ms. Fincastle instead.

Ms. Fincastle was *seriously* into the names on those sticky notes—one was so funny that she snorted a little.

Audrey L was surprised that happened to grownups too.

So she was one million percent sure Ms. Fincastle would like Cha-Cha Domino the most.

Or Beluga.

Or maybe Moonrock.

"All righty, mighty sand crabs," Ms. Fincastle walked to the board with a handful of sticky notes and a bright blue marker. "You all had *stupendous* ideas, but I narrowed down the choices to my top five. That's called a *teacher perk*."

Audrey L could have sworn Ms. Fincastle smiled right at her when she said that.

"Your *student perk* is that if you win—if your classmates vote on your name for our new friend— you will get to take him home for the weekend. Of course, you'll have to be a very, very, very responsible scientist. Promise?"

"Promise!" Room 19 yelled.

Ms. Fincastle's handwriting mesmerized Audrey L— it was so neat, like she had typed it on the whiteboard.

Audrey L even added a clickety-clackety sound in her head, the same kind the keyboards made in computer class. She crisscrossed her fingers in her pockets and *hope-hope-hoped* one of her names would be called.

But when Ms. Fincastle was finished writing names on the board, this was the list:

Swirly-Q
Henrietta
King Crab
Ms. Pinchcastle
Squirmy The Hermie

None of Audrey L's had even made it into the top five.

And when Room 19 had finished voting—heads down, thumbs up—it looked like this:

Swirly-Q	3
Henrietta	1
King Crab	2
Ms. Pinchcastle	8
Squirmy The Hermie	4

Ms. Fincastle looked super-duper starry-eyed to have a hermit crab named after her.

The only person who looked happier was Audrey W. She must have invented that name.

Audrey L was equal parts jealous and in complete awe.

CHAPTER 18

When Audrey woke up on Saturday morning, she smashed each of her stuffed animals into a pile around her head. Most weekends, she popped out of bed like warm, crunchy bread fresh from the toaster. But second grade had been really hard work that week.

"Hey, Audrey! Help me in the kitchen?" Mom yelled up the stairs. "Bakers have to be prepared."

Audrey pretended not to hear.

But Mom was still talking. "Ms. Fincastle didn't ask *me* to be the Welcome Ambassador! That's *your* job, Audrey!"

Well that was true.

Audrey was definitely excited to have Audrey W come over to her house. Having somebody see your baby pictures and your bare feet and your annoying little brother means they are an actual, real friend.

So Audrey pulled herself out from the stuffed animals and opened her door. She had to step over Bobo to walk down the stairs.

"Fine, but there are rules," she said. "Nothing with sunflower seeds, blueberries, or oats."

Audrey meant business.

"And NO tongs."

"Perfect," said Mom. "Those things sound kind of wrong for a cake anyway. And all we really need is a spatula to get every last lick from the bottom of the bowl. No tongs."

Audrey and Mom hustled and bustled and busied themselves—floofing pillows, stuffing clutter in the closet, finding *sticker-quiet* activities for Bobo, and washing all the baking spoons.

"It will be fun to have Audrey W over, right?"

There was no way Mom knew Audrey had thrown away the printer-paper note or had wished she'd squeezed harder on Audrey W's pinky, just enough to pinch for a split second.

"Bettina probably would have done a better job as Welcome Ambassador," Audrey said, her belly flip-flopping with the truth. "I'm barely even an okay friend."

"Wrong!" Mom said, pulling Audrey close. "You are an excellent friend —the very best!"

"Mom," said Audrey. "How would you even know? You're a *mom*, not a friend."

"Okay. I'll stick to just being Mom. But that means I know exactly how lucky your friends are to have you. So there, Jellyfish." Mom kissed Audrey on the forehead and let her eat her scrambled eggs alone.

After breakfast, Audrey wrote a new note on a piece of regular old printer paper.

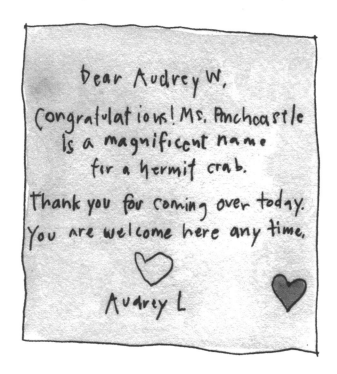

Dear Audrey W,

Congratulations! Ms. Pinchcastle
is a magnificent name
for a hermit crab.

Thank you for coming over today.
You are welcome here any time.

♡

Audrey L   ♥

CHAPTER 19

When the doorbell rang, Bobo was the first to the door. Audrey L was close behind. She had to make sure he didn't flick boogers at somebody who might be kind of friend-ish.

"Hi! You must be Bobo!" Audrey W said, smiling like he was the most darling boy in the whole wide world.

She obviously didn't have a little brother.

Right then, Bobo turned himself into a robot. He made his eyeballs extra big and beep-booped and made weird moves with his arms and legs.

"Hi, Other Audrey! I'm This Audrey's dad, but you'll have to excuse me while I go polish a robot. It's

cleaning day!" Dad scooped up Bobo in his arms and they both beep-booped their way up the stairs.

"Come on in, Audrey." Mom dodged Dad and Bobo to sneak in a hello. "We're so happy to have you!"

"Yeah," said Audrey L. "We won't even make you clean that robot. Just the kitchen! Mom doesn't care about a mess as long as we get it squeaky-clean after."

"Clean kitchens make food taste better!" Mom said, disappearing up the steps behind Dad and Bobo.

"Here. Let me help." Audrey L grabbed one of Audrey W's backpack straps while she wiggled out of it. She could tell marshmallows were in there because marshmallows were the only treat you could smell through their plastic bag. It was like they wanted to ooze out and be delicious, ready or not.

"Thanks," said Audrey W. "Your family is funny. Bobo is so cute!"

Most of the time Audrey L thought that Mom and Dad and Bobo were ANNOYING and EMBARRASSING and WEIRD. They definitely did unusual things like hang Dad's constellation socks on top of the Christmas tree instead of an actual star every year. But Audrey W was right. They *were* funny—and weird, but in a good way. She was happy Audrey W felt right at home.

"That's the truth," Audrey L said.

Audrey W also held a plastic tank with a plastic handle. Ms. Pinchcastle!

"I thought she'd like to come too." Audrey W was using both hands and stepping on one of her feet with the other. Ms. Pinchcastle scuttled along the bottom of the tank.

"Ms. Pinchcastle definitely seems excited about this," said Audrey L. "Now come on. We've got work to do."

"Whoa," Audrey W said when she saw everything.

"Yeah," said Audrey L. "We like to bake in this house. It was Mom's thing at first, but I've gotten pretty good at it too."

"You've even got one of those fancy mixers," said Audrey W. "It kinda looks like a robot."

"Oh, no," said Audrey L. "Don't even say that! Bobo is totally and completely not allowed in this kitchen!"

Audrey L and Audrey W unpacked the backpack and organized the sprinkles in rainbow order. They set Ms. Pinchcastle on the counter, away from the island, away from the mess. She'd have a good view from there too.

Then Audrey W pulled out a pouch shaped like an alicorn from her backpack. It was purple and glittery and had some loop-dee-doops on the sides. The loop-dee-doops were scratching off a little, probably because it had been stuffed into her backpack so many times.

That's how it is with special things.

"I drew the wings myself," Audrey W said. "Alicorns are the best."

"I know," said Audrey L.

Not many people understand about alicorns, she thought.

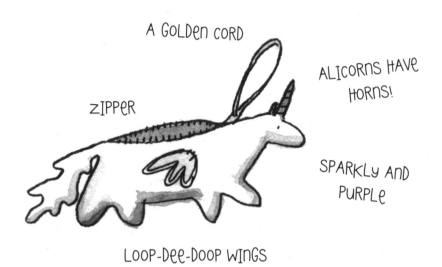

A GOLDEN CORD

ZIPPER

ALICORNS HAVE HORNS!

SPARKLY AND PURPLE

LOOP-DEE-DOOP WINGS

When Audrey W unzipped the alicorn, she dumped out nine bottles of nail polish—a few shades of lavender, some silver, a pale green, and one hot pink with sparkles.

Audrey L knew they'd both pick a purple.

CHAPTER 20

"Do you ever watch the show *That's So Sweet*?" asked Audrey W. "It's my favorite. Want to play it?"

It was Audrey L's favorite show too. The answer was an obvious "YES!"

That's So Sweet! was a show on TV where cupcake decorators competed and this super-famous dessert lady, Mavis Ellison, was the judge. She wore giant eyeglasses and always tucked a flower behind one ear. And she'd say things like *Deeeelicious!* and *Deeeeelightful!* and *How am I supposed to pick a winner from all of these mmmmmmasterpieces?*

At the end of the show, the bakers shared all their treats. Everyone laughed and sampled and taste-tested and it was one big party. Mavis Ellison picked a favorite, but everyone tied for the best. Audrey L liked that a whole, whole lot.

"Okay!" said Audrey L. "First, we need to bake."

"Well, first," said Audrey W, "we need to have a challenge, right? Like a main idea?"

"Let's do cupcakes. Have you ever seen anything more adorable than a cupcake?"

"Never," said Audrey W. "And you can eat like four of them before you start to feel sick."

"Want to know a secret?" Audrey L teetered carefully on the stepstool and pulled down all the tiny bowls. She hated doing the dishes, but all the bakers on *That's So Sweet!* kept even the teensiest dashes of cinnamon in itty-bitty bowls. "I sorta like the baking and decorating parts better than the eating part. All that goo, that beautiful goo—remember?"

"We're flip-flop opposites," said Audrey W. "I loooooove the eating part the most!"

"Well, it sounds like we are a perfect team," said Audrey L.

She helped Audrey W with the measuring and mixing and pouring. They didn't even need to ask Mom for help with the robot on the counter. Because Audrey L was an expert.

Once all the batter was plopped into place, they set a timer for eighteen minutes on the dot, then they practiced their crisscross jump rope outside. Of course, Audrey L let Audrey W use the purple one. She'd won it in first grade when she'd guessed the number of bouncy balls in Coach Mallory's truck.

He'd replaced a bunch of busted ones, so he made the first graders practice their estimation. There were sixty-three bouncy balls and Audrey L guessed sixty-two. She'd been the best at *something*, once upon a time.

"Were you the only Audrey at your old school?" Audrey L asked.

"Yep," said Audrey W as she crissed and crossed.

"Same," said Audrey L.

"But I don't mind the W thing," Audrey W said. "Do you?"

Audrey L thought and thought and thought. She *did* mind the W thing.

But she said, "No," and that made Audrey W smile.

Audrey L hadn't seen that kind of smile yet. It was wider than when they'd been glockenspiels and different around the eyes than when Audrey W had won Team Fincastle's Drumstick Championship. It wasn't really even on her face at all when she'd laughed with Bettina at the fire drill. Audrey W's smile was even better than a laugh. Maybe it was the kind of look real friends share?

"It was different back there," said Audrey W. "I always had to stand in the back row for our class pictures next to doofuses like Jax and Andy. All because I'm tall! And last year, when I wrote a secret pal note on our alicorn stationery, Ruthie O'Connell said believing in alicorns was for babies."

"Oh, no," whispered Audrey L.

"And sometimes I took chocolate-covered crickets for snack, so everyone said my lunch box was full of germs."

"Oh," said Audrey L.

Audrey L hadn't thought of things that way before.

"So when I heard we were moving, I was definitely ready to find some friends." And then Audrey W went right back to crissing and crossing.

No, Audrey L hadn't thought of things that way at all. She hadn't realized that Audrey W had *also* been just plain Audrey before.

Except being just plain Audrey wasn't a big deal to Audrey W. To Audrey W, being Audrey W meant she had an instant team, a pal, a friend.

Their name was something she liked to share.

"Hey!" said Audrey W. "We'll need a judge for *That's So Sweet!*, right?"

"Dad!" said Audrey L. "He is the very best taster, believe me."

And then Audrey W got the giggles.

"You have a funny laugh! It sounds just like a dolphin!" said Audrey L.

"I know!" said Audrey W.

"But Audrey! We are beluuuugas, not dolphins!" Audrey L said, feeling a dolphin-giggle overtake her too.

"Your dad doesn't look anything like Mavis!" Audrey W could hardly catch a breath.

"But he is an expert at *mmmmmmasterpieces*! And Mom has the best flowers," Audrey L waved her hand toward Mom's garden. Dad would have his pick of colors.

"I'm so glad Ms. Fincastle made me a beluga," Audrey W said in between gulping laughs and wiping her face for funny-tears. Laughing and crying at the same time was definitely the kind of thing real friends share.

When they finally heard the kitchen timer buzz, Audrey L and Audrey W dashed back inside to pull their cupcakes out of the oven.

"Don't forget the pot holders!" Mom called from someplace else.

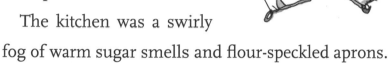

The kitchen was a swirly fog of warm sugar smells and flour-speckled aprons.

"Your mom lets you do this part by yourself?" Audrey W asked.

"Yeah. She's been teaching me since I was Bobo's age. Okay, put this pot holder on the hand you use the most." Audrey L gave Audrey W the one with chili peppers on it. It was her favorite. "You can open the oven and I'll pull out the cupcakes."

"Got it," said Audrey W. "You're so good at this!"

When Audrey W carefully opened the oven door, Audrey L reached in with the yellow-striped pot holders and pulled out the cupcake tin. She freed a finger and gently touched one golden cupcake. It was poofy on top and perfectly springy.

"That's how you can tell if they are finished." And then Audrey L turned off the oven.

"They smell amaaaaaaazing," Audrey W said.

"They have to cool for a while and then we can decorate them! And then—the PARTY."

"Um, Audrey?" Audrey W froze in place. "We've got a problem."

"The sprinkles are over there, remember?" Audrey L turned and pointed.

But Audrey W didn't say anything.

Earlier, each of the nine nail polish bottles had been lined up on the counter like an itty-bitty rainbow next to Ms. Pinchcastle. But now there were only eight.

And Ms. Pinchcastle was gone.

"MS. PINCHCASTLE!" Audrey L shrieked.

"Oh, no. This is *not* how to be a responsible scientist!" Audrey W knocked over a bowl of sprinkles. "I'm in huge trouble."

The sprinkles scattered bumpity-down all over the floor, popping and bouncing like the party had already started.

But it definitely hadn't.

Ms. Pinchcastle was missing!

CHAPTER 21

The girls skipped super quick out of the kitchen. Audrey L grabbed a wooden spoon just in case she needed to scoop up a crab.

There were not many suspects on the list.

Mom.

Of course not.

Dad.

No way.

"BOBO!"

Audrey L and Audrey W ran up the stairs.

The door to Bobo's room was closed but not locked. Bobo had not been allowed to lock his door ever since the Yogurt Incident.

Audrey L pushed open the door and yelled, "WHERE IS MS. PINCHCASTLE?"

Bobo turned around s u p e r - d u p e r - d u p e r s l o w l y. His hands were empty. Both Audreys felt a small puff of relief . . . until they saw his fingernails.

Hot pink. With sparkles.

"Bobo," Audrey W said, so nicely, so big-sisterly. "Your nails look awesome. But—"

"WHERE IS SHE?" Audrey L put on the meanest face she'd ever used. Still, she used some common sense about stomping because she did NOT want to crunch Ms. Pinchcastle.

Bobo didn't say a word, but he couldn't help it. He was only four. He looked toward the windowsill.

And there was Ms. Pinchcastle. She was tippity-tapping her way along the sunny ledge, and she was hot pink. With sparkles.

CHAPTER 22

Audrey L wished they were back to crisscrossing or nail polish or anything else while their cupcakes cooled. Audrey W's best-friend-ish smile was long gone. At least Ms. Pinchcastle was safe in her plastic crate, sitting on the coffee table.

Audrey L pulled at a thread on one of the pillows. She remembered when she'd twisted a button loose and plucked it right off the pillow the night before second grade started, and Bobo had gotten in trouble for it. She'd felt bad at the time.

Not anymore.

"Ms. Fincastle is going to be so, so, so, so, so angry." Audrey W slumped her shoulders, but she didn't cry.

Maybe you shouldn't have brought Ms. Pinchcastle over here is what Audrey L thought. But she didn't say it, not quietly or yelling, because neither was very welcoming. Or best-friend-ish.

"Remember when Ms. Fincastle messed up? With the spelling tests?" Audrey L said. *She* certainly did. "Maybe we can make her a note. Or a picture, like she made me. Or a friendship bracelet?"

"Maybe we can take her some cupcakes?"Audrey W said. "We're still going to decorate them, right?"

"Oh, yeah," said Audrey L. "When Goldie brought in her birthday donuts, Ms. Fincastle scraped off all the icing with a plastic knife. She ate that part and threw away the donut bottom. She will *love* what we do with frosting."

"Did you know you're still holding that wooden spoon?" Audrey W asked.

Audrey L and Audrey W laughed together. It wasn't the same as before, but she saw a little sparkle back in Audrey W. Audrey L felt bad—it was her fault that Audrey W had lost some of her sparkle in the first place. This wouldn't have happened at Audrey W's house. Bobo wasn't *her* brother. Maybe she wished she had just stayed home.

"How's it going, girls? Feeling okay, it sounds like?" Mom's voice at the door made Audrey L drop the thread on the pillow. Mom still thought Bobo had pulled the button loose.

"Not exactly," Audrey L said, nodding toward Ms. Pinchcastle. "Bobo did it."

"Oh," Mom said. "Well, this is a bit of a problem, isn't it?"

"We're going to give Ms. Fincastle our cupcakes," Audrey W said.

"She loves frosting more than a friendship bracelet," Audrey L added.

"I love how you're thinking of Ms. Fincastle, but we've got to think about Ms. Pinchcastle right now,"

Mom said. She looked more bummed than she had about the button. "Why don't you girls decorate your cupcakes, and I'll see if Mr. Min is around."

Since this was sort of an emergency, it was pretty lucky to have a neighbor like Mr. Min because he was a veterinarian. It definitely helped more than Henley or the seventeen cats.

"And, Audrey? *My* Audrey? You'll have to take some responsibility for this too. It's not all Bobo's fault, you know. So be thinking of what to say to Ms. Fincastle."

Mom must know all about being *a responsible scientist*.

"I know, Mom. It's the best thing to do." Audrey L was an expert in best things, even if she wasn't ever any of them.

"Don't worry," Audrey L said to Audrey W while they headed back to the kitchen. "Mr. Min is like a library if the library *only* had animal books. And if a library was a person. He'll help us."

Even though their sugary spirits were down in the dumps, Audrey W and Audrey L still had work to do. Back in the kitchen, Audrey L decided on a design.

She turned her cupcake into the weird fried egg from their stationery.

It was *not* a weird egg anymore. It looked super-duper-duper awesome. The white part was made out of Marshmallow Fluff and the yellow part was all sunshine-colored chocolate that smooshed around like clay. Audrey L even used only the black sprinkles so it looked like pepper.

It looked so delicious, so real—like if you didn't see its cupcakey bottom, you'd think it was a salty, slimy, crunchy, breakfast-time egg.

Audrey L remembered that Audrey W loved Marshmallow Fluff, so she'd definitely love it.

And Dad (Mavis!) would call it a *mmmmasterpiece!* She'd totally win.

Ms. Fincastle would be mind-boggled that even a true creative talent could figure out a way to use that much frosting.

It was perfect.

And Audrey W? She tried her best.

She piped polka dots around the edge and made a swooshy-swirl of hot pink in the middle. Audrey L thought it was supposed to be Bobo's version of Ms. Pinchcastle. Either way, it was maybe a disaster.

Audrey L knew hers was much more *deeeelicious* and *deeeeelightful* than Audrey W's. Still, she said, "Good job!" to Audrey W, and she meant it.

Bobo and Dad hopped into the kitchen, hypnotized by the aroma of cupcakes and competition. They each had a flower behind one ear.

"Ooooh," Dad said when he had a bite of the one that looked like Ms. Pinchcastle.

"Aaaah," he said when he ate the egg.

"Mmm," Bobo said when he found a green sprinkle on the floor.

"So I'm supposed to pick a favorite here?" Dad asked. "That's what Mavis does, right?"

That was true. It was the whole point of Audrey W's visit, wasn't it?

Even though *technically* everyone tied, Audrey L wanted to have the best cupcake. She wanted to win.

Audrey L and Audrey W held hands because of the suspense.

"Okay," Dad said. "One million points for this egg! I can't believe it's not breakfast!"

If Dad had a filing cabinet, Audrey L's fried egg would go right on top. (Unless he ate it first.)

"One million!" Audrey W squeezed Audrey L's hand. Audrey L felt like one million bucks.

"And for this—this pink swirly explosion!" Dad said. "One million and *fifty* points!"

Audrey L couldn't believe it.

Dad had picked Audrey W's cupcake to win.

Bobo cheered. Mom cheered.

This was SO NOT SWEET.

And it was SO not very welcoming or best-friend-ish, or even nice when Audrey L yelled to Audrey W, "I WISH YOU NEVER CAME TO ROOM NINETEEN OR MY HOUSE AND YOU LAUGH LIKE A DOLPHIN AND I DIDN'T VOTE FOR 'MS. PINCHCASTLE' ANYWAY."

She stomped upstairs, curled up in a bunch of blankets, and let the tears that had been building up all week run down her face like sprinkles of sadness.

And even though she was mad and sad and everything in between, all she could think about was that she'd just left Audrey W in the kitchen with her own annoying, embarrassing, and weird family.

Now Audrey L knew what she was the best at. She was the best at wrecking friendships that had barely even had time to become *stupendous* yet.

CHAPTER 23

It could have been hours or days or *centuries* since Audrey W left.

The other Audrey.

The brand-new Audrey.

Audrey L had wanted to be Audrey again—just plain Audrey.

Now she was just Audrey, alone.

And that didn't feel good either.

Mom knocked at her door and peeked in. She was quiet and gentle about it, as if Audrey was a cream puff who would deflate if you opened the oven too early.

"Hey, Jellyfish." Mom brought in a tray with bowls of soapy water, yellow washcloths, and Ms. Pinchcastle.

"You're in charge of Ms. Pinchcastle now. Audrey W agreed that you could take over until Monday. And Mr. Min said we could try this to clean her up a bit. Scoot over."

Mom swirled a washcloth around in the soapy water and handed it to Audrey. While Mom held Ms. Pinchcastle like a fragile eggshell, Audrey dabbed the hot pink away. Ms. Pinchcastle's legs dangled a little at first, but then she tucked them up inside her shell.

"Will she be okay?" Audrey asked. "She's as special as Ms. Fincastle."

"Mr. Min seemed to think so. It's not a good idea to paint a hermit crab's shell, especially when they're still inside. You wouldn't want paint to flake off in your food, would you? But she should be okay."

Ms. Pinchcastle was as cozy as Audrey in the blankets. But she didn't have friends in her plastic crate.

Audrey knew what that was like. She and Diego dressed up as spaghetti and meatballs for Halloween last year. Diego had worn a mop on his head. She was the meatball.

"Mrs. Waters came to pick up Audrey," said Mom. "And you know what? Audrey picked *your* cupcake to take home with her. It was her favorite. *You* are her favorite."

"Of course she did, Mom," said Audrey. "She was just being nice."

"Maybe," said Mom. "I think you're both nice."

"We're flip-flop opposites," said Audrey, but she kept thinking. "Even though I guess we did jinx *twice* already."

"Twice? Well, that's a sign of true friendship." Mom squeezed her close. "But I'd think about what friends do after a mix-up." Mom left Ms. Pinchcastle on Audrey L's desk.

Just Ms. Pinchcastle, alone.

Audrey opened her purple stationery.

The only pieces left had alicorns on the bottom.

She sat up straighter.

It was time to write the most important letter of her life, and now she had the most perfect paper to write it on.

Dear Audrey W,

Remember the first time I wrote you a note on our favorite purply stationery? I picked the piece with the fried egg on the bottom. I thought it was weird.

Back then I didn't even know you yet or want to be your Welcome Ambassador and so I definitely didn't want to use my MOST FAVORITE piece with the alicorn on it.

Now I wish I had.

I'm sorry for not locking Bobo in his room. And I'm sorry for lying.

I DID vote for Ms. Pinchcastle. It was my most favorite name (out of the ones that I didn't make up). I can't picture Ms. Pinchcastle as a Squirmy The Hermie, can you?

Love,
Audrey L
I think YOU'RE SO SWEET!

And since she had one more alicorn, she wrote another note. This one was to another favorite person, another alicorn type of person.

Dear Ms. Fincastle,

First, let me tell you that Ms. Pinchcastle is JUST FINE!

Well, you will know that already by the time you are reading this, but I am trying my very best to be a responsible scientist.

I'm sorry.

Also, thank you for choosing me to be Audrey W's Welcome Ambassador. You must have known how much we have in common. You must have known we were both ready for a friend.

Nobody should be all alone in a plastic crate.

Your student,
Audrey L

CHAPTER 24

On Monday morning, Dad and Audrey left for school reallllly early again because of the trash truck. But smelling the back of a garbage truck sounded even better than getting to school early.

"How are you feeling, Cupcake?" Dad looked through the rearview mirror.

"Don't call me that," Audrey said.

"Okay," Dad said. "How are you feeling, Regular Cake?"

"*Pianissimo*, Dad," Audrey said.

Neither one said anything through four stoplights.

"Hey, Audrey?" Dad said at the fifth. "I should have called a tie on the cupcakes. I'm sorry."

Audrey looked at the two cupcakes in her lap. One was decorated to match Ms. Pinchcastle's pink shell, and one looked like a fried egg—a magnificent, stupendous, *not*-weird fried egg.

"No, Dad," said Audrey. "She should have won. Besides, can you believe this color? She didn't even bring pink frosting over. She mixed vanilla with some squirts of red and the squishy strawberries Mom left out for us. It's magnificent! It's stupendous! It's amazing! Audrey W is a true creative talent."

"One million extra points to you, Audrey." Dad's eyebrows crinkled up with a smile. "You should tell her. Friends need reminders like that sometimes."

Inside, the hall was pin-drop quiet all the way to Room 19. Diego's early bus wasn't even there yet. But as Audrey L got closer and closer and closer, she heard laughing. Ms. Fincastle didn't usually laugh before she finished her gigantic black-as-night iced coffee, and it was way too early for that.

Audrey L had never had to apologize like this before. But she'd never had a best friend.

First, Audrey L taped her note to the inside of Audrey W's cubby.

Then Audrey L took a deep breath of *here we go* and walked into Room 19. She had Ms. Pinchcastle's tank under one arm and a container with two cupcakes in the other.

Someone else *was* already there before the early bus, before Diego, and before Audrey L.

It was Audrey W.

"Hi," said Audrey L. It was a start.

"What an adventurous weekend you've all had!" Ms. Fincastle took her glasses off her head and slipped them on the right way to take a closer look.

Ms. Pinchcastle looked mostly the same, but there was still one faint pink swoosh along her swirly shell.

"I'm really sorry, Ms. Fincastle."

"What happened?" Ms. Fincastle sounded pretty sure that she didn't have the whole story.

"It was Bobo," said Audrey L.

"It was an accident. We were at Audrey L's, baking and crisscrossing and having the best time ever." Audrey W scooted closer to Audrey L.

What was happening? Audrey L had said the meanest things to Audrey W. She had even STOMPED AWAY. But Audrey W scooted closer.

"We were going to paint our toenails, but Bobo found the nail polish first. We shouldn't have kept it so close to Ms. Pinchcastle," Audrey L said.

"Believe me," said Ms. Fincastle. "I've seen much worse when it comes to accidents and little brothers. Looks like Bobo is an *arteest*!"

"You might want to retire before he gets to second grade," said Audrey L.

Ms. Fincastle didn't say anything for a minute. Was she thinking about retiring right then and there?

"You know Mr. Min, the veterinarian?" Audrey L couldn't help but blurt it out, like always. "He said she'd be okay, and he told us Animal Kingdom would have everything we need. I don't really know what he means."

"Okay, well," Ms. Fincastle said. "Why don't you two stay in during morning recess? You can figure out what to do for Ms. Pinchcastle. I trust that you are responsible scientists."

Audrey L couldn't believe Ms. Fincastle wasn't that mad. And she couldn't believe Audrey W had scooted closer. She wasn't mad about the stomping and the yelling and the cupcake and Ms. Pinchcastle?

Audrey W was acting exactly like a friend. No *ish* about it.

CHAPTER 25

Audrey L couldn't wait for morning recess, even though she and Audrey W had to stay in because they were in trouble—*ish*.

They had a problem.

They had a deadline.

They had each other.

When the rest of the kids bolted out of the room, Audrey L and Audrey W cozied up with a pile of books and Ms. Pinchcastle.

"Okay, so we've got to find the page about how hermit crabs swap old shells for new ones," Audrey W said.

"Got it," Audrey L flipped forward and back and forward and back in her book.

"Look, Audrey," said Audrey W. "Use the big words to help."

Audrey W pointed to LEGS AND MORE LEGS and TIDAL POOLS AND TROPICAL PLACES. She even flipped to the index. Audrey L sorta kinda remembered learning about the index in first grade.

The list sounded like a poem.

baby hermit crabs

breathing

claws

plankton

predators

shells

Audrey L made a plan to write that poem on printer paper for Ms. Fincastle's filing cabinet later.

"Right here—page twenty-two," said Audrey W. "Baby hermit crabs choose small shells for their first homes. As they grow and grow and grow, their shells get tight and it is time to move. A bigger shell becomes a new home."

"Mr. Min was right," said Audrey L. "Ms. Pinchcastle will be okay in her painted shell for a little while since she'll have to move anyway. We'll just get her a new one!"

"Right!" Audrey W said. "Remember how I brought sunflower seeds and blueberries and oats? This book is how I knew what to feed a crab. Your hints were a huge help."

"Oh," Audrey L said.

"I thought it would be a welcoming thing to do for the newest member of Room Nineteen, just like my Welcome Ambassador made me an alicorn cake." She nudged Audrey with her elbow, leaning in close.

Audrey L's belly was all fizzly. She still hadn't all-the-way apologized to Audrey W—for the cupcakes, Ms. Pinchcastle's name, anything. What if she changed her mind about being a friend?

Now Audrey L's heart was pounding so much, she could *truly* feel the burn. So she ran to the bathroom as fast as she could. It was most definitely an emergency.

CHAPTER 26

Audrey L locked herself into the first bathroom stall. It was the very best thinking spot.

She wasn't the best at saying sorry.

She wasn't the best at fixing mix-ups.

And if she wasn't the best at being a friend, how could she be a *best* friend?

After a while, the next-door-stall opened and closed. Audrey L spotted the coolest sneakers with bright ink splotches along the edges.

"Audrey?" Audrey W said. "Recess is over."

The only noise in the bathroom was the leaky sink.

"Can you come back? Ms. Fincastle said to partner up, and I could really use my favorite glockenspiel."

Drip, drip, drip went the sink.

If Audrey L didn't go back to class, Audrey W might have to be the third ukulele to Wesley and Mimi. Audrey W would be left over.

"Audrey?" Audrey W said again.

"I've never even been somebody's favorite glockenspiel," Audrey L said. "I mean, I'm hardly ever somebody's partner. I'm always in the leftover trio. We were only a table of three Beluga Whales before you came, and Diego always picked Henley."

"Did you know that belugas have a lump on their heads called a melon?" Audrey W asked.

Audrey L wasn't too sure what melons had to do with glockenspiels, but she did *not* know that about belugas. And then she was ready to apologize.

"I was so mad at Dad when you left that I threw one of your cupcakes in the garbage can and it landed on green beans so it was completely ruined because they were slimy and kind of brown," Audrey L said. "I'm sorry I couldn't save it. It was a masterpiece. You are a true creative talent."

"Really?"

"Definitely."

"Well, we made a bunch, right? Maybe Bobo accidentally put some boogers in that one anyway."

Bobo probably hadn't. But that was an amazing thing for Audrey W to say.

"And," said Audrey W, "did you also know that belugas and narwhals are in the same family? And narwhals are basically unicorns in the ocean, right? They've got a horn instead of a melon!"

"Are we ocean unicorns?" Audrey L asked.

"That's reallllly close to an alicorn!" Audrey W's ankles rolled back and forth under the stall door. "Audrey?"

"Yeah?"

And then Audrey W stuck something underneath the bathroom stall. It wasn't toilet paper. It was way better.

Both Audreys were quiet for a minute.

Then there was a tap-tap-tappety-tap. It was the ink-splotched shoes. Audrey W was drumming on the floor. And s l o w s l o w s l o w l y, Audrey L joined in.

Pretty soon the bathroom was a racket of the best kind of stomping. Bobo could not have banged out a better tune with his pots and pans.

"Do you feel the burn, HEY-HO?" asked Audrey W.

"I feel the burn, LET'S GO!" answered Audrey L.

Before either of them could say anything else, a booming voice echoed into the bathroom. Mrs. Getty, the fourth-grade teacher—who everybody wanted for a teacher but nobody wanted for an enemy—yelled, "GIRLS! This is a place for *business* and *business* only! Flush down, wash up, hustle out!"

"You know what that means," Audrey L whispered once she was pretty sure Mrs. Getty had *hustled out* herself.

"*Pianissimo!*" Audrey W whispered back. Then she stretched her pinky finger under the stall. Audrey L pinky-pinched right back.

Then they took the long way back to Room 19.

Audrey L walked a little funny on purpose, like she'd sprained an ankle. If a teacher fussed at them for wandering the hall, it would look like Audrey W was helping her to the sickroom.

And then Audrey L could say, *Isn't this what friends are for?*

"Your cupcake really was delicious," said Audrey W. "I knew it would be, because anyone who can make a pile of alicorn poop look scrumptious is somebody I want to be *best* friends with."

Audrey L felt like an alicorn was fluttering across her heart.

Nobody had ever said anything like that to her before.

"I'm really sorry I threw yours away," said Audrey L.

"I'm really sorry you had to eat slimy green beans," said Audrey W.

"And also, I'm really sorry I got so mad that you knew about Ms. Pinchcastle before me," said Audrey L. "It didn't seem like you'd need me for a friend if you've got all the good secrets already."

"Audrey!" said Audrey W. "Who else has not laughed ONE SINGLE TIME about chocolate-covered crickets being disgusting? Or would share their purple jump rope and use the one with the broken handle instead? And who else would have jinxed TWICE already?"

"Definitely NOT Bettina," said Audrey L, and she scooted closer to Audrey W. "There's nobody else I would want to get in trouble with, other than you," she said.

But there was more than that.

"Remember the spelling test?" she continued.

"You're the only person besides Ms. Fincastle who has ever said I *rock*. And once, Bettina barfed when I tried to teach her how to play Washing Machine. But you didn't. And finally, finally, finally there is somebody else in Room Nineteen who is a true creative talent. Your pink frosting was the best I've ever seen. That color was like a summer sunset plus a super-silky alicorn mane plus the pink gelly pen that I used to have before Bobo lost it. I loved that pen."

Audrey W looked at Audrey L like she was the most important thing in the world. This must be what it was like to be seen by a true, true friend. It was the best feeling.

"Audrey?" said Audrey W. "I'll ask my mom if we can go to Animal Kingdom tonight to get stuff to save Ms. Pinchcastle."

"Wait!" Audrey L said. "Animal Kingdom is right by Pizza Bernal. We always go there on Monday nights.

You have to come. Usually Diego eats with us, but you'll sit next to me, right?"

"Obviously!" said Audrey W. "We can be in the same pod at a new table. Promise."

"Okay," said Audrey L. "What do you think beluga whales eat on their pizza?"

Then, two friends snickered and skittered, fake-hobbled and pinky-pinched, all the way back to Room 19.

CHAPTER 27

Mom, Dad, Bobo, Audrey L, and Audrey W pulled into the Animal Kingdom parking lot. It was a quick stop on the way to Pizza Bernal.

Audrey L had never had a partner for Monday-night pizza before.

"We'll wait here, okay? Be quick, or Diego will have eaten already and won't be able to join us." Mom handed Audrey L a whole twenty-dollar bill and didn't even ask for the change.

"Okay then, we'll go slow!" Audrey L said.

"Hey, Beluga Whales stick together, remember?" Audrey W reminded her.

"Can I go? I want a guinea pig!" Bobo unbuckled his seatbelt.

"No, Potato. The girls have some homework to do." Dad twisted around to see Bobo. "Want to play I spy?"

"I spy something invisible!" Bobo said.

This could take a while, Audrey L thought. "Let's go," she said.

Animal Kingdom smelled like someone had forgotten to clean the hamster cage again. But Audrey L and Audrey W were on a mission, and stinky sawdust would not stop them.

"Okay, so shells. Shells, shells, shells," Audrey L said. "They're probably by the water things, right?"

"What aisle are the fish in?" Audrey W said.

"Aquatic Creatures—Aisle Eight!" Audrey L spied a sign hanging from the ceiling.

Audrey W grabbed Audrey L's hand and off they went.

Audrey L knew what *aquatic* meant. She knew that *aisle* had a homophone.

And most especially, Audrey L knew she had a friend.

The girls passed Habitats and Hutches

and Scratching Posts

and Dinosaur Eggs

and Reptile Hammocks

and Fig and Insect Gecko Treats.

They were getting closer to the Aquatic Creatures when Audrey L spotted something sparkling on the other side of a birdcage. Inside was a squawking bird with a mohawk who would not stop caw-caw-cawing. But just past that bird, something glittered like one of Ms. Fincastle's headbands. And when they heard a lady say, "Look at this little pup!" Audrey L and Audrey W looked right in each other's eyeballs.

It was absolutely, positively, definitely Ms. Fincastle.

"Do you think she's making sure we are responsible scientists?" Audrey L whispered.

But Ms. Fincastle wasn't checking up on her little chickens.

She wasn't thinking about Audrey L and Audrey W one eensy bit.

That's because she was with . . .

Mr. Min.

"Who is *that*?" Audrey W pressed her face as close to the birdcage as she could get without sticking her nose inside. "Wow. They must be realllly good friends."

"That's Mr. Min!" Audrey L said. "Ms. Fincastle is HOLDING HANDS WITH MR. MIN."

Mr. Min wasn't even wearing his veterinary scrubs. He had a sweater on, the kind that Mom made Dad wear to Aunt Bea's wedding. And Ms. Fincastle was even wearing contacts instead of her glasses. She never wore those at school.

It was super-duper-duper weird.

"Audrey," said Audrey L. "What if they GET MARRIED? What if Ms. Fincastle moves in next door?"

Audrey L couldn't tell if she really, really wanted that to happen or really, really, REALLLLLY did not.

When Ms. Fincastle and Mr. Min went one way up their aisle, Audrey L and Audrey W went the other. They did NOT want to see any more of that hand-holding. And what if Ms. Fincastle asked if they had finished their homework?

Finally, they made it to the Aquatic Creatures aisle. They passed a bunch of fake logs and colorful pebbles and fish food in a giant bucket. There was even a whole wall of tropical-looking backgrounds you could pick for your fish to feel like they were on vacation.

Right where Aquatic Creatures turned into Small Reptiles, Audrey L and Audrey W spotted a warm, bright tank with six beautiful shells scattered around. Most were sleeping, but one was scuttling around in his cozy pile of wood chips. Next to the crab-walkers and crab-sleepers, there was a big bin of empty shells. They were swirly and spotty and pearly and dotty and came in a bunch of different sizes. It was like the sea had spit up its prettiest shells in one big burp. Audrey L knew they would find the best one for Ms. Pinchcastle.

"Hey, Audrey—look!" Audrey L stuck one shell on each of her fingertips. "What do you think about this nail polish?"

Audrey W laughed. *"Stupendous!"*

And then she couldn't stop.

She stuck five shells on her own nails, and it was way better than any nail polish she had in her alicorn pouch.

Then Audrey L and Audrey W marched around in the Aquatic Creatures aisle together.

"Everything okay over here?" A big kid with a name tag that said *I'M NATE. MY FAVORITE ANIMAL IS A RED PANDA* did *not* seem to like what he saw.

"Yes, umm," said Audrey L. "What aisle are the red pandas in?"

Nate shook his head and kept on feeding fish, but Audrey W got the dolphin-giggles again.

Then Audrey L and Audrey W dug through the shell box for the very best treasures.

"Too tiny!"

"Too boring."

"Hey, what about this one? It's like a perfect swoosh of frosting, right?" Audrey W asked.

"See, I told you," said Audrey L. "True creative talent."

Then they picked out three more of the best shells. Their research said hermit crabs like to choose which one they like best. And since they had twenty whole dollars, Ms. Pinchcastle would get some options.

CHAPTER 28

Pizza Bernal was super-duper-duper crowded. It always was.

"PIE-FIVE, Belugas!" said Diego when Audrey L walked in with her entire family AND Audrey W.

Diego always saved their favorite booth, the big maroon one in the back. It belonged to Diego and the Lockes, even on nights when Henley's family came in first, and Henley had four brothers.

But tonight—finally—they had enough people to fill it up. That's what one best friend does.

"How was your day, Diego?" Dad knew Diego always had the best stories. "Anyone lose a tooth in music class?"

"Not today," said Diego. "We finished the game of Instrument Twin that the fire drill ruined last week. I had to be a sand block with Goldie."

"A sandbox?" said Bobo.

"A sand block. Like this." Diego rubbed his palms together real fast until they got all heated up. "Be Goldie, Bobo!"

Bobo did.

"Interesting!" said Dad.

"And how about you girls?" Mom asked. "What were you?"

"Well, does this give you a hint?" Audrey L picked up her spoon and clang-a-langed it against her water glass.

It didn't sound much like a glockenspiel, but it was kinda close.

"Beautiful!" Mom said, laughing. "What about you, Audrey?"

Audrey W picked up her own spoon and matched Audrey L's dinging.

"We are the glockenspiels!"

And then it was all fhh-shh-shh and ting and tang and Bobo making inappropriate noises with his mouth because that was more fun than a pretend sand block. It was the best party.

Finally, Mr. Bernal came over with two giant pizzas. "Can I interest this symphony in some pizza?" Mr. Bernal knew what to put in the oven as soon as the

Lockes walked through the door. He was definitely a stupendous Welcome Ambassador.

"Thank you, thank you," Dad said, spinning the green pepper half closer to him.

When the pepperoni-only half was closer to the girls' side of the table, Audrey L and Audrey W pulled two steaming slices apart until the stretchy cheese split.

"Did I tell you one of the names I thought of was Pepperoni? Can you picture Ms. Pinchcastle as a Pepperoni?" Audrey L scrunched closer to Audrey W.

"JINX!" said Audrey W. "I wrote Pepperoni too!"

Turns out Ms. Fincastle was wrong.

Audrey L and Audrey W had more than *one* particular thing in common—they had one billion little things in common.

And one billion little things add up to make one best friend.

MS. FINCASTLE'S LITTLE CHICKENS

Dear Room 19,

November is coming!

WHOOOO's ready?! (Thank you for that funny joke, Diego!)

Remember when we talked about what it means to be nocturnal? We definitely can't sleep all day and party all night here in Room 19, but you've formed some very strong opinions about a class sleepover.

Here's the deal, take it or leave it. (That's another teacher perk!)

If we write a letter to Mrs. Louis to ask permission . . .

And if Mrs. Louis says yes . . .

Then we can have a half sleepover. Let's call it a halfover. Your grownups will have to get you at 9:00 p.m.!

You'll need to pack a pillow.

You'll need to practice your talents.

You'll need to be ready to party half the night.

Until then, here are your November jobs! Since we will be extremely busy, nobody is on vacation. It's teamwork time, little chickens!

Line Leader: Goldie
Librarian: Audrey L
Paper-Passer-Outers + Collectors: George + Jamie
Most Responsible Scientist: Audrey W
Plant Waterers: Lena + Charlie
Assistant Coaches: Kadir + William
Mini Ms. Fincastle: Diego
Computer Technician: Isabella
Street Sweeper: Mimi
Newscaster: Sage
Caboose: Wesley
Recycling Boss: Sonya
Litterbug: Von
Postal Clerk: Henley
On ~~Vacation~~ Halfover Helper: Bettina

Love,

Ms. Fincastle

PS: Have you seen my glasses?